TEENAGE MUTANT NINJA TURTLES®

THE MOVIE

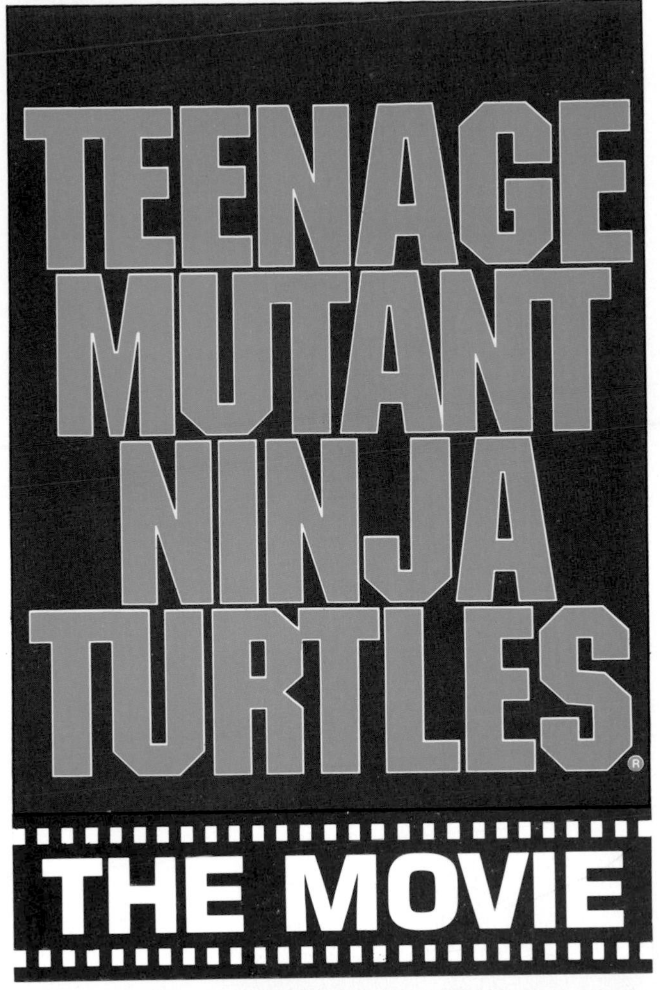

STORYBOOK WRITTEN BY GREG STEDDY

Hippo Books
Scholastic Publications Limited
London

Based on the film
TEENAGE MUTANT NINJA TURTLES
– THE MOVIE –

Scholastic Publications Ltd.,
10 Earlham Street, London WC2H 9RX, UK

Scholastic Inc.,
730 Broadway, New York, NY 10003, USA

Scholastic Tab Publications Ltd.,
123 Newkirk Road, Richmond Hill,
Ontario L4C 3G5, Canada

Ashton Scholastic Pty. Ltd.,
P O Box 579, Gosford, New South Wales,
Australia

Ashton Scholastic Ltd.,
165 Marua Road, Panmure, Auckland 6,
New Zealand

Published in the UK by Scholastic Publications Ltd., 1990

ISBN 0 590 76468 3

Made and printed in Belgium

10 9 8 7 6 5 4 3 2 1

It was night and an air of brooding menace hung over the city like a dark shroud. People were scared — and they had every reason to be. For weeks a wave of organised crime had been sweeping, unchecked, through the city and the authorities seemed powerless to stop it. Only one person had the courage to speak out in public against the unknown villains — plucky young April O'Neill, crime reporter for the Channel News.

She had just finished her nightly News Bulletin and was crossing the darkened car-park to her car, when she walked right into a group of young thugs stealing equipment from a nearby news van.

"Bad timing, lady," sneered one of the thugs, drawing a knife. Before April had a chance to defend herself, they had bundled her roughly to the ground.

Suddenly, a small dagger smashed into the street lamp above their heads, plunging the whole scene into darkness. Four powerful figures leapt silently out from the shadows and within seconds April's attackers were lying in a dazed and battered heap on the ground. Then, as swiftly as they had arrived, her rescuers were gone.

April picked up the odd-looking dagger and looked at it curiously. Little did she realise that she had just had her first encounter with the Teenage Mutant Ninja Turtles!

Beneath the streets, the Turtles returned to their secret hideout in triumph.

“Gimme three, brothers!” cried Michaelangelo, grinning broadly. “Man, we were awesome!”

“Major league!” chuckled Leonardo. ‘Quite excllent!”

Their master, Splinter, the wise old rat, nodded in approval as the Turtles eagerly related the story of their first real fight.

"But tell me, were you seen by anyone?" he asked anxiously.

Leonardo shook his head.

"Be sure of this at all times," continued Splinter. "For even our allies would not understand. You must strike hard and fade away — without a trace!"

"Master Splinter," interrupted Raphael, looking dejectedly at the ground. "I lost one of my daggers up there. But I can get it back. I know who has it."

"You must let it go," said Splinter firmly, but softly. "I know it is hard for you down here. Your young minds are eager, but you must never stop practising your ninja skills. Always remember this."

Raphael shrugged. He was still angry with himself for losing his dagger and just felt like being on his own for a while. He pulled on a trenchcoat and hat and quietly slipped out.

★★★ ★★★

Raphael was walking through the park when he came across a young masked vigilante beating two hoodlums senseless with a hockey stick.

"Hey, cool it, pal," said Raphael. "These guys have had enough."

"Chill out, weirdo," said the stranger. "No-one speaks to Casey Jones like that! Besides, these scumbags need a lesson."

"Not like that, they don't," said Raphael, dumping Casey on the ground. "This town's rough enough as it is."

"Man, you're crazy!" gasped Casey, as Raphael stalked away. "And dangerous!"

★★★ ★★★

Chill out, weirdo!

The following evening the Turtles were watching April O'Neill's latest TV news broadcast on the crime wave.

"The latest information we have," she reported, "is that these crimes are being organised by a mysterious clan known as The Foot — a secret band of highly trained Japanese warriors!"

"Isn't she wonderful?" sighed Michaelangelo, gazing dreamily at the screen.

Right on, sister

"Perhaps the most disturbing aspect of this whole business," continued April, "is that the police and the city authorities seem unable, or unwilling, to do anything about it!"

The Turtles were so engrossed that none of them saw Raphael slipping out, with a purposeful look on his face.

★★★ ★★★

April, meanwhile, finished her broadcast and made her way to the underground station. Missing the train by seconds, she found herself alone on the platform. Or so she thought!

Suddenly, a band of hooded men in black jumpsuits leapt out of the shadows and surrounded her. It was the dreaded Foot Clan!

"Your mouth may yet bring you much trouble, Miss O'Neill," hissed their leader menacingly. "We're here to shut it for you!"

The man struck her hard in the face and she fell unconscious to the ground.

Fortunately for April, help was near at hand. Raphael, still determined to recover his lost dagger, had also been following her.

With a terrible roar, he leapt into the middle of the Foot like a cyclone, scattering them like ninepins.

Swiftly scooping April up in his arms he dived across the tracks just before a train pulled into the station. He disappeared silently into the maze of tunnels he knew so well, little knowing that one of the Foot was following him . . .

RRROAARRR

"Raph, are you crazy?" snorted Leonardo, as Raphael gently laid the still unconscious April on the couch in the Turtles' hideout. "Why bring her here?"

"She was mugged on the station," said Raphael defensively. "What else could I do?"

"We must help her," said Splinter, gently stroking her forehead with a cold flannel.

Gradually April's eyes flickered open as she began to come round. At the sight of Splinter and the Turtles bending over her, she let out a scream of terror.

"Oh my god!" she babbled. "I'm dead, aren't I? No, wait. I'm dreaming. That's it. Those guys in black pyjamas hit me — and I'm still unconscious. I . . ."

"Calm yourself, Miss O'Neill," said Splinter soothingly, "and I will explain everything."

"That's perfect," groaned April, sinking back onto the couch. "It talks too!"

"Many years ago," began Splinter, "I was a pet of my master, Yoshi, a wise Japanese warrior. Soon after we were forced to come to this city, I found myself alone and without a home. One day I witnessed a terrible road accident. A lorry swerved in the road and shed its load of metal canisters. One of these bounced into a crowd of onlookers and hit a glass jar carried by a small boy. In the jar were four baby turtles.

"Guess who?" grinned Michaelangelo.

"The turtles were covered in a glowing chemical from the canister and fell down a manhole into the sewers," continued Splinter. "I cleaned them up as well as I could, but, to my amazement, over the next few days they began to grow! I too was growing, in mind as well as in body and I began to train them, teaching them all I had learned from my master, Yoshi. Soon, they could not only speak, but had also mastered the fighting skills of the ancient Ninja warriors. So may I now introduce you to your rescuers — Leonardo, Michaelangelo, Donatello and Raphael."

Leonardo

Michaelangelo

Donatello

Raphael

April was speechless. It had been a long and eventful day, but this was starting to get too weird.

"Listen guys," she said shakily. "Thanks for your help and everything — but if you don't mind, I think I'd like to go home and lie down for a while."

"No problemo, sister," said Michaelangelo. "We'll take you the pretty way!"

The Turtles led a bemused April through a maze of tunnels, finally emerging from a manhole right outside her apartment.

"Er, I'd invite you in," said April hesitantly, "but the place is a mess — and all I've got to offer is frozen pizza."

In a blur of green the Turtles were suddenly lined up expectantly by her door.

"You guys eat *pizza*?" said April weakly.

"Doesn't everybody?" grinned Michaelangelo.

Fresh from the sewers

Back in the safety of her own apartment, April started to relax a little. Michael-angelo made them all laugh with his impressions — and she actually found herself enjoying the company of these eager green youngsters.

"Come on, team," said Leonardo finally. "We'd better be going. Splinter will only worry about us."

Reluctantly they said goodbye to April and made their way back to their hideout. But there a terrible sight met their eyes. The whole place had been ransacked and there was no sign of Splinter anywhere — just a trail of blood leading from his chair.

Raphael howled in anguish and sank to the floor in despair. "This is all my fault," he wailed. "I must have been followed back here!"

"You weren't to know, Raph," said Leonardo gently. "Let's go back to April's — she may be our only hope!"

★★★ ★★★

Overcome by the loss of their beloved master, the Turtles sat up all night with April, trying to work out their next move.

As the sun came up the following morning, a loud knocking at the door startled them all into action.

"Er, who is it?" asked April uneasily.

"It's me, Charles," said a voice. "We need to talk."

"It's my boss!" whispered April urgently. "You guys had better hide!"

Charles Pennington walked into the room looking worn and harassed, followed by his son, Danny.

Charles was in an awkward fix. The day before, Danny had been arrested for shoplifting and the police chief had agreed to let him go on one condition — that Charles's crime reporter should stop openly criticising the police over the Foot Clan business.

"Listen, April," began Charles, hesitantly. "I've been thinking — maybe you should drop this Foot case for a while. I mean, look at you — you look terrible."

"I've just had a rough night, that's all," said April flatly. "Besides, this is *my* case — and I'm going to crack it, you'll see."

Whilst they were talking, Danny was wandering idly around the apartment. Suddenly he caught sight of a strange green reflection in a mirror. When he looked again to double check, it had gone.

"Well, just take it easy, will you," said Charles. "That's all I'm asking. Come on, Danny, we'd better be off."

Danny followed Charles out, still thinking about what he thought he'd seen. It was crazy, but it had looked like a giant green turtle . . .

On the other side of the city stood a large warehouse. From the outside it looked perfectly ordinary, but inside it was home to hundreds of the city's wayward adolescents — the dregs of urbanization. There were groups of them idling everywhere — smoking, drinking, gambling, playing pool. To these young outcasts and delinquents, the warehouse was paradise. All round the place, boxes of stolen goods were piled high. Here and there, groups of youths could be seen working out to improve their performance on the streets or practising the martial arts.

Walking slowly between the various groups of youngsters was the burly figure of Tatsu, a vicious brutal man who watched over his charges with a rod of iron, demanding fear and respect with every glance, every footstep.

Suddenly, a door swung open and a deathly silence fell over the whole gathering. A tall menacing figure in a long black cloak strode towards a raised platform, his piercing eyes staring coldly through the slit in his metallic helmet.

"Make way for Master Shredder!" commanded Tatsu respectfully.

"We have a new enemy," hissed the Shredder, glaring at his silent audience. "Freaks of nature who interfere with our business. You must be my eyes and ears. Find them. Together we will punish these creatures — these *turtles*!"

A murmur of approval ran through the rows of teenagers. One of them suddenly opened his eyes wide in recognition. Turtles! Then he *hadn't* imagined it!

"We already have their leader," gloated the Shredder nastily. "Behold, this pathetic rodent!"

A badly beaten and exhausted figure was dragged forward and chained in front of them. It was Splinter! Danny Pennington rose slowly to his feet and raised his hand nervously.

"M-Master Shredder," he stammered. "I know where to find the turtles . . ."

Back in April's apartment, the Turtles were watching April's latest TV report about the Foot menace.

Suddenly Raphael got up and turned off the set angrily.

"We can't just sit here doing nothing!" he exploded. "Splinter's out there, remember?"

"What *can* we do?" snapped Leonardo. "April's our only link with these Foot guys. We have to wait till she comes up with something!"

"Oh, brilliant!" scoffed Raphael. "And that's the best you can do? Well, I'm going outside — maybe I can think of a better idea!"

He stormed out and sat moodily on the roof of April's apartment block, staring down at the traffic below. He was so preoccupied that he failed to notice a band of Foot creeping up silently behind him . . .

The rest of the Turtles were watching cartoons when April returned home.

"Any news, April?" asked Donatello eagerly.

"Not yet," she replied, "but I've told them to call me here immediately anything turns up."

"Thanks, April," said Leonardo, trying not to sound disappointed. "We really appreciate it, you know."

"Forget it," said April. "Hey, where's Raphael? I was going to show you guys round my junk shop downstairs."

"He, er, went out for a while," said Donatello, looking quickly at Leonardo.

Little did they know that on the roof, Raphael was fighting for his life. He was heavily outnumbered by the Foot and they were giving him a savage beating.

"Are you sure he's OK?" asked April uneasily.

"Don't worry," said Donatello reassuringly. "He does this all the time. He *likes* it!"

"Yeah," grinned Michaelangelo. "He'll probably be back with some major notion any minute now!"

The words had barely left his lips, when Raphael was hurled bodily through the window and landed with a sickening crash on the floor.

"Raph! Speak to me!" cried Leonardo, rushing to his side.

"Is he . . .?" began April, unable to finish the sentence.

"No, he's alive," said Leonardo grimly. "But only just!"

Suddenly the remaining windows were shattered and dozens of the Foot began to swarm into the apartment.

"And I thought insurance salesmen were pushy!" said Michaelangelo through clenched teeth. "Come on, dudes, let's rock!"

While April tried to shield Raphael, the other three Turtles charged into their attackers, laying them out on all sides.

"Hey, don't knock 'em *all* out, guys!" cried Leonardo. "We'll need one of them to tell us where Splinter is!"

"No problem, Leo," said Michaelangelo grimly. "Here comes the second wave!"

More and more Foot began to burst in, some carrying heavy ninja battleaxes. As the fight raged all around, the floorboards in April's apartment started to creak.

Suddenly with a great snapping and splintering sound the whole floor gave way and everyone tumbled headlong into the junk shop below. As the dust cleared, the Foot started to drop down through the gaping hole in the ceiling.

"Man, we could really do with Raph right now," muttered Leonardo, raising his swords wearily.

As if in answer to his prayer, the masked figure of Casey Jones burst in off the street, his hockey stick at the ready.

"If you've hurt my little green pal over there," he roared, pointing at Raphael, "you'll have Casey Jones to answer to!"

"Who on earth is that?" asked Leonardo in disbelief.

"Beats me," shrugged Michaelangelo, "but he seems to be on *our* side!"

The Turtles and Casey attacked with renewed vigour, until a flying axe severed the main power cable in a shower of sparks. All the lights immediately went out and flames started licking up the wall.

"We've got to get out of here!" cried Leonardo, as the fire took hold.

"This way," shouted April. "There's a hidden exit behind these shelves!"

With Casey covering them from behind, the Turtles and April dragged Raphael through a half-door and disappeared. Casey was just about to follow them when April's phone rang and her answering machine clicked on.

"April, this is Charles," said a voice. "Look, I don't know how to put this — but you're fired. Sorry, April."

Casey shrugged and bolted the door behind him. He leapt into his battered old truck, with the Turtles and April hidden in the back, and drove off, as the sound of police sirens filled the air.

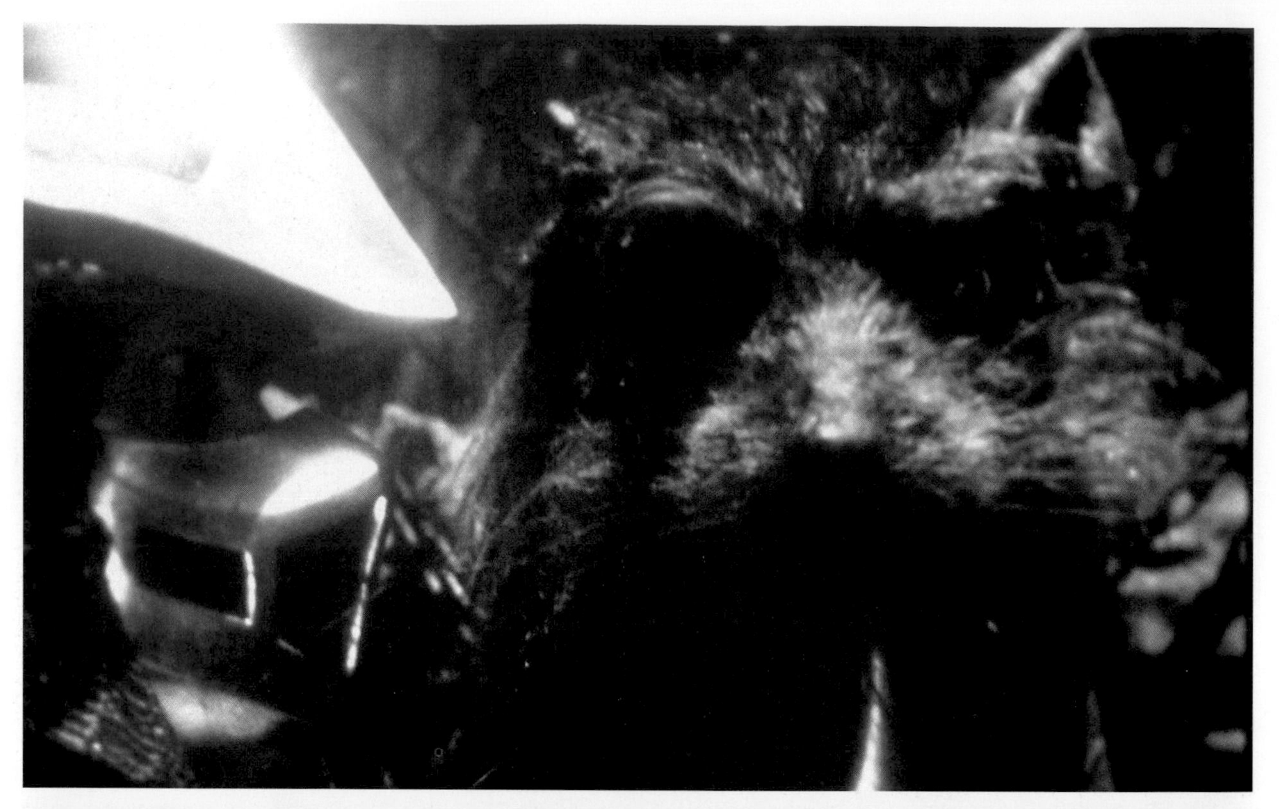

Back at the warehouse, the Shredder was white with rage as his defeated army returned in disarray. He strode towards the manacled Splinter and gave him a vicious backhand across the face.

"Who *are* these freaks?" he stormed. "How do they know how to fight like this? Answer me!"

But the brave old rat merely gave a slight smile and remained silent. The Shredder stalked off in fury.

Danny Pennington wandered along

deep in thought. He had just witnessed the terrible carnage outside and knew deep down that he was partly to blame. He stood for a moment in front of Splinter and a troubled look came over his face.

"How can a face so young wear so many burdens?" asked Splinter gently.

"So you *can* talk," said Danny, peering closely at the old rat.

"Yes, and I can also listen," said Splinter. "My ear is open — if you care to use it."

"I don't think so," said Danny slowly. "I need time to think."

Splinter watched him go with sadness in his eyes.

As dawn came up the following morning, Casey's truck rattled to a halt in front of a ramshackle old farmhouse way out in the country.

"Sorry about the mess," said April apologetically. "This place used to belong to my grandfather and I haven't been out here in years!"

"Well, the van's had it anyway," sighed Casey. "The engine just died."

"Great!" snorted April. "Then I guess I'll just have to *walk* to the nearest phone. I need to let my boss know where I am."

"Er, not necessarily," said Casey awkwardly. "He left a message on your answerphone. You're fired!"

April's mouth dropped open in amazement. "Well, thanks a bunch, pal," she snorted. "What do you do, take classes in insensitivity?"

"Just trying to break it to you gently," muttered Casey, as April stalked off.

★★★ ★★★

The farm was to be their home for many days. Leonardo kept a constant vigil by Raphael, who lay stomach down in the bath, watching anxiously as he made a slow and painful recovery from his terrible ordeal.

Donatello found a new ally in Casey, as they passed the time tinkering under the bonnet of the truck, cheerfully trading insults.

Michaelangelo seemed to burn with a furious intensity, training alone and working out in the barn day after day.

April spent the time recording all this in her diary and making sketches of her new friends. Losing her job was hard to take, but she knew it was nothing compared to the Turtles' loss. Without Splinter they were not whole and she could feel this almost as keenly as they did.

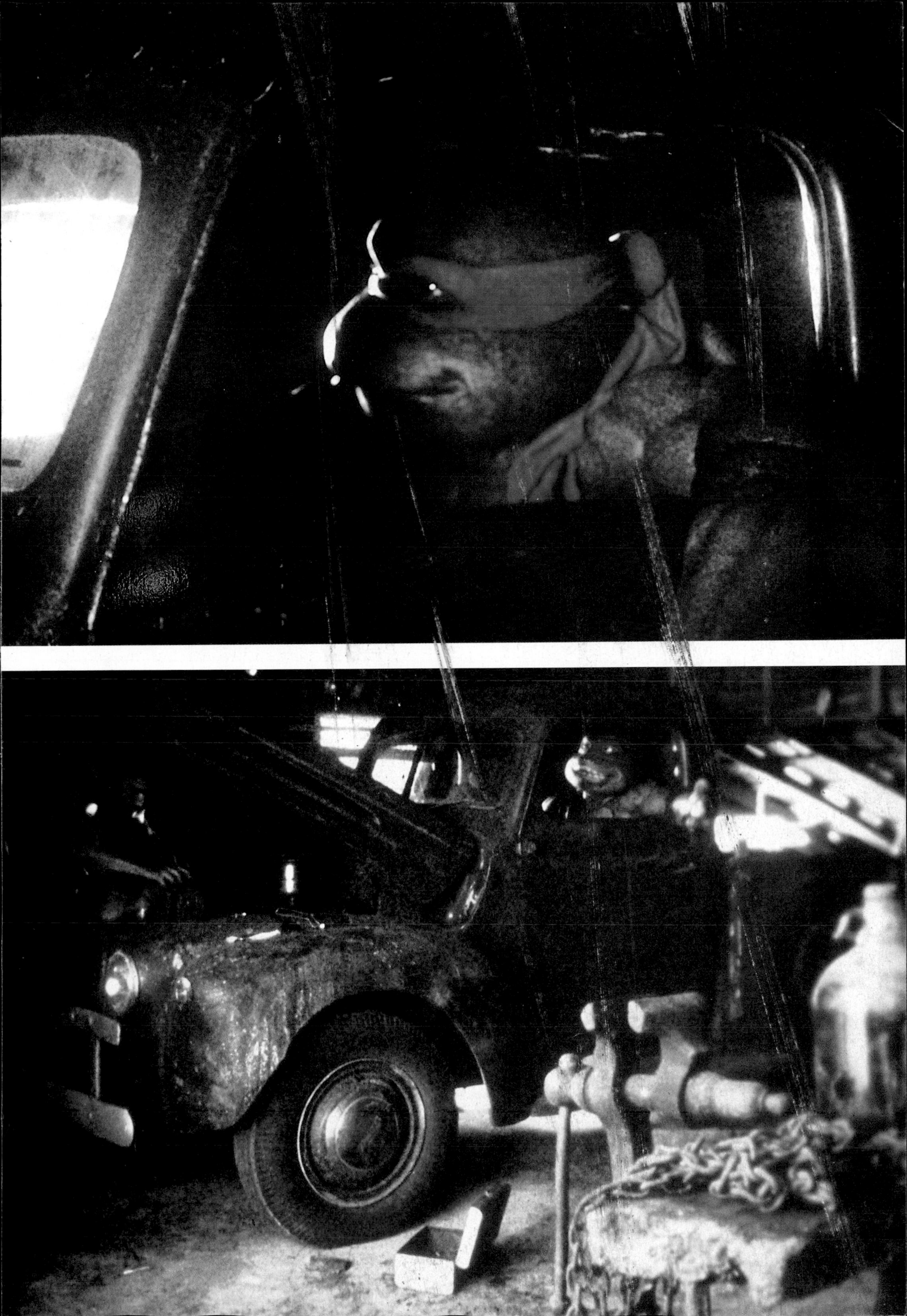

Turtle Power!

Good news came when Raphael was well enough to get up. The Turtles were a team again. Yet the burning question remained — where was Splinter?

Leonardo would spend hours meditating alone in the woods. One day, as he sat deep in thought, he heard a voice, the merest whisper, calling his name. He sat bolt upright and sprang to his feet.

"He's alive!" he cried, racing back to the farmhouse to tell the others. "Splinter's alive!"

"Of course he is, Leo," said Donatello gently. "We all *think* he's alive."

"I don't think," said Leonardo passionately. "I *know*!"

Later that night the four Turtles sat expectantly round a fire in the woods.

"Leo, if you've dragged us out here for nothing . . ." said Raphael.

"Just close your eyes and concentrate," said Leonardo seriously.

Nothing happened for some time, but gradually a faint image of Splinter began to form in the flames.

"I am proud of you, my sons," said the rat softly. "Tonight you have learned that ultimate mastery comes not of the body — but of the mind. Together there is nothing your minds cannot accomplish. Help each other. Remember the true force that bonds you. Remember too, I love you all, my sons."

The image then faded and the Turtles sat together for a long time in silence, filled with wonder at what they had just seen and heard.

From that moment on, the Turtles trained with a new intensity, working on their skills day and night and developing their strengths to levels previously untried. Finally, when they were completely satisfied, they looked at each other in silence and nodded. This time they were ready. There was no doubt about it.

"What's with you, guys?" asked April, as the Turtles stood before her fully armed, looking grim and determined.

"It's time to go back," said Leonardo simply.

Leaving the farm behind them, the Turtles returned to the city with April and Casey and made their way to their home in the sewers.

Casey looked around in disbelief. The place was still as the Foot had left it.

"This is just great," he snorted. "First it's the farm that time forgot and now this! I guess you can't get decent maid service down here!"

"Quit complaining, dude," chuckled Michaelangelo. "It's only for one night."

A sudden noise from one of the cupboards froze them all in their tracks. With weapons drawn, the Turtles flung open the door and leapt forward.

"Danny!" gasped April in surprise. "What are *you* doing here?"

"Don't shoot!" whimpered Danny, backing into a corner. "I ran away from home, that's all."

"Your dad must be worried sick," scolded April. "I'll call him right away."

"No, please don't!" Danny whined. "Let me stay here, just for tonight?"

"Sure, kid, you can have my place," said Casey. "This joint gives me the creeps. I'm going to sleep in the truck!"

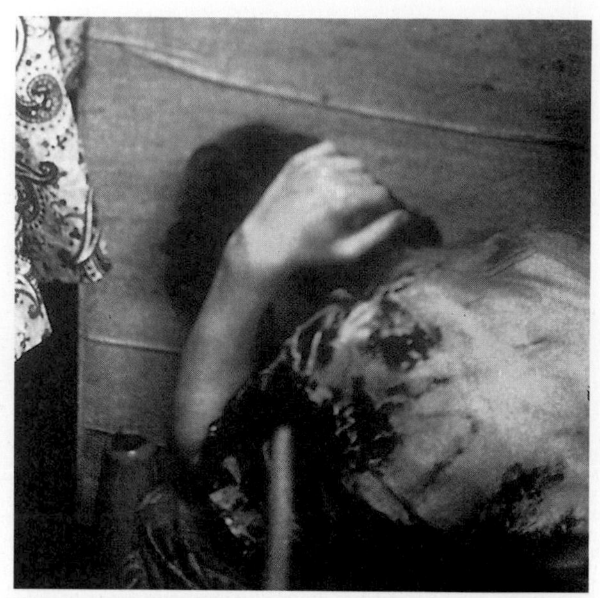

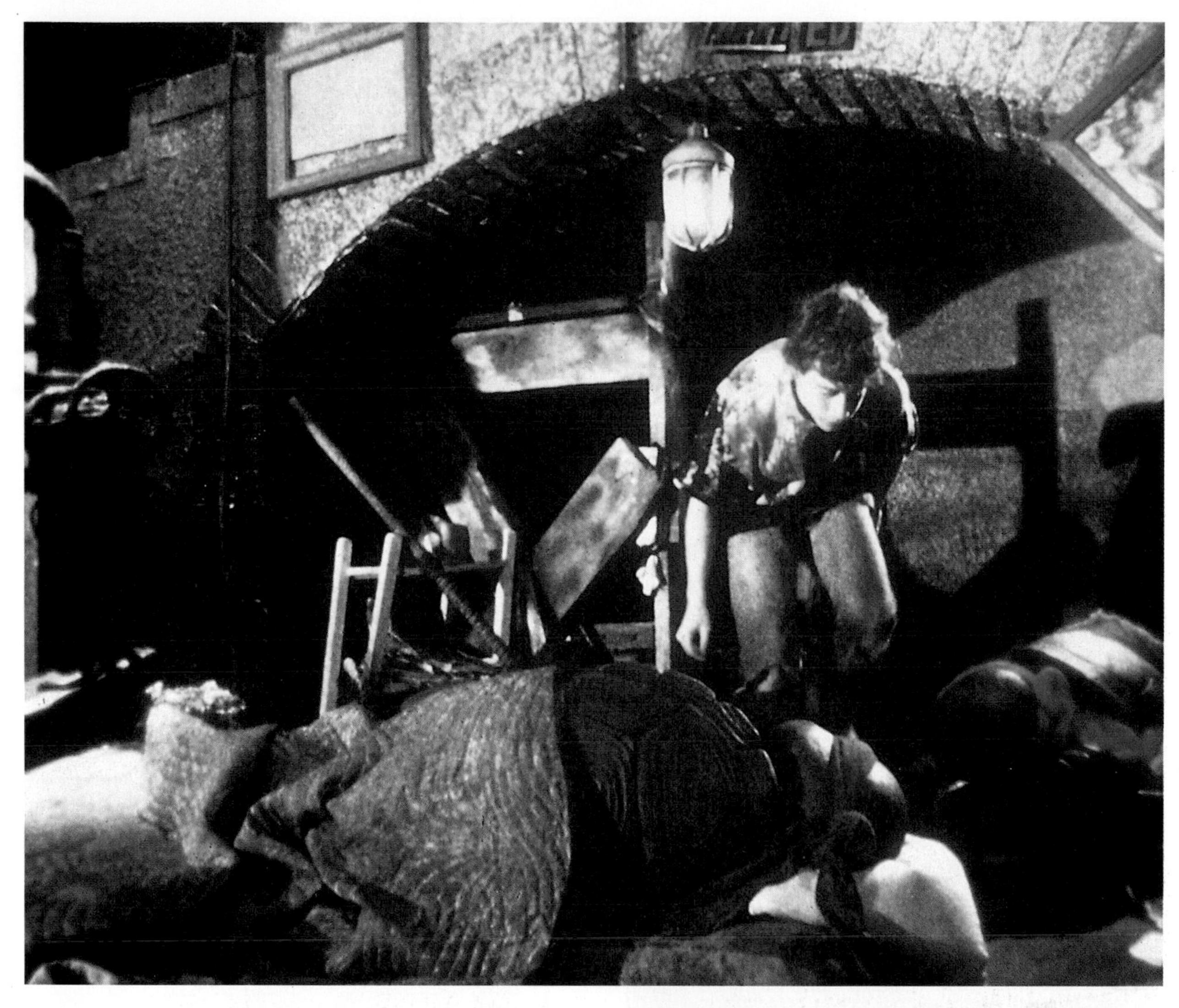

Once the Turtles and April were asleep, Danny rose silently, removed a few of April's sketches from her pad and tiptoed outside. Casey, still trying to get some sleep in the truck, watched him go and followed him stealthily across town until they came to the warehouse. Pausing only to tie on a headband, Danny slipped inside, with Casey hot on his heels.

Danny wandered around the warehouse until he came to the spot where Splinter was still held captive.

"I have not seen you for many days," said Splinter weakly.

"I've been at my hideout," Danny replied.

"So you now hide from your adopted family here as well as from your father?" asked Splinter.

"I don't know," sighed Danny. "I wish I knew what to do."

"I once had a family," began Splinter. "I lived in Japan with my master, Yoshi, a great Ninja warrior. He had a great rival called Oroku Nagi and they both loved the same woman. Nagi was jealous of my master and they fought for the woman's love. By accident, Nagi was killed.

We fled here to America, but Nagi's younger brother, Oroku Saki, swore vengeance on my master. He trained hard and was full of hatred, becoming the most feared Ninja warrior in Japan.

One night my master returned to find his beloved woman lying dead. Saki had returned and killed her. I leapt at Saki's face, biting and scratching with my claws, but he threw me aside, slicing my ear with his sword. My master was no match for the wrath of Saki and soon he too lay dead — and I was alone."

"Whatever happened to this Oroku Saki?" asked Danny, listening with interest to Splinter's story.

"No one really knows," said the rat slowly, "but you wear his symbol on your headband!"

Recognition dawned in Danny's eyes, as he suddenly realised the true identity of the Shredder. He slowly untied the headband and dropped it to the floor, his mind finally made up.

A cold, harsh voice stopped him in his tracks.

"What are you doing there, boy?" asked the Shredder, stepping forward with his henchman, Tatsu.

"N-nothing, Master," stammered Danny, trying to conceal his terror.

"You're lying," snarled the Shredder, "and you're hiding something as well."

In an instant he snatched April's sketches from Danny's pocket and studied them closely. He turned to Tatsu with a triumphant glint in his eye.

"They're back," he breathed. "And this time there will be no mistakes. I shall go myself!"

He turned on his heel to go and then stopped.

"Tatsu," he hissed malevolently. "The rat — kill it!"

Within minutes the whole warehouse was a hive of activity, as the entire army of Foot prepared for the final onslaught.

In all the confusion Danny managed to slip away unnoticed — somehow he had to help Splinter!

Suddenly, an arm reached out and dragged him behind a pile of boxes. It was Casey.

"So there you are," cried Casey angrily. "You've got some explaining to do, you little . . ."

"You've got to come with me," gabbled Danny breathlessly. "They're going to kill Splinter!"

They had just managed to remove Splinter's chains when Tatsu arrived. Casey stepped forward to face him, but was knocked backwards by a lightning punch. He picked himself up, but was sent crashing into a pile of boxes. He shook his head groggily, as his eyes focussed on what he'd landed on — a pile of stolen golf equipment!

Tatsu moved in for the kill, but Casey swung a driver in a glittering arc, exploding with a crack on Tatsu's jaw and knocking him out cold.

"Who says golf's a dull game?" he grinned, swaggering back to Danny and Splinter. "Come on, guys, the show's over. Let's get out of here."

Meanwhile, dozens of Foot were invading the sewers from all sides in a desperate attempt to flush out the Turtles. They burst headlong into their hideout but, to their surprise, there was no sign of the Turtles or April anywhere.

Suddenly an unseen green hand switched on all the steam valves and the Foot were thrown into confusion.

With a fearful roar, the Turtles leapt into battle, and soon the Foot were flying in all directions.

Take out the garbage

"Looks like these guys are suffering from shell shock," chuckled Michaelangelo, whirling his flails to deadly effect.

"For sure, brother," grinned Donatello, weaving past on his skateboard and flattening a group of Foot with his staff. "I guess we can really shell it out!"

Leonardo and Raphael drove the remaining Foot up the tunnel and the battle spilled out onto the street.

The Turtles chased the remnants of the Foot army up a fire escape and onto a roof for the final showdown.

Suddenly a sinister figure leapt down from a higher rooftop and landed in their midst.

"Who on earth is that?" said Leonardo, stepping backwards.

"Search me," said Michaelangelo, noticing the figure's vicious armour, "but I bet he never has to look for a can opener."

"You fight well," hissed the Shredder, "but you've caused me enough trouble. Now you face the Shredder!"

"The Shredder?" echoed Michaelangelo. "You mean all that hardware's for making coleslaw?"

We're ready for you, Shred-head

The Turtles leapt at the Shredder, but soon realised that they'd met their match. Michaelangelo picked himself up shakily and dusted himself down.

"Er, guys," he ventured, "at exactly what point did we lose control here?"

"Whoever he is," muttered Leonardo, "he must know where Splinter is."

"Ah, yes,the rat," gloated the Shredder. "I know exactly where he is. We just killed him!"

"You lie!" roared Leonardo, and flew at the Shredder in a blind rage.

"Mistake, freak," hissed the Shredder, disarming Leonardo and moving in for the kill.

Radical rat

"Saki!" commanded a voice.

The Shredder spun round to see Splinter standing before him, his eyes glowing with fire.

"Yes, Oroku Saki. I know who you are," said Splinter grimly. "We met many years ago — when you killed my master, Hamato Yoshi!"

"You!" snarled the Shredder, removing his helmet to reveal deep scars on his cheek. "Then I will finish what I began with your ear!"

He let out a howl of pure hatred and charged towards Splinter with his staff. At the last minute, Splinter whipped out a flail and wrapped it round the staff, tipping the Shredder over the edge of the roof.

The Shredder hung on grimly, his eyes wide with terror.

"Death comes for us all, Oroku Saki," said Splinter gravely, "but something much worse comes for you."

The Shredder reached desperately for a small dagger and with a final despairing effort, hurled it at Splinter.

The rat shot out a hand and caught the knife, releasing his hold on the flail at the same time. With a terrible scream, the Shredder disappeared over the edge and plummeted downwards.

"For when you die," whispered Splinter, "it will be without honour!"

As the Turtles rushed up to Splinter and flung their arms round him, the police began to round up the rest of the dazed Foot below. The whole area looked like a bomb had hit it. April crawled out of the sewers and went over to join Danny and Casey as a crowd began to gather.

At that moment, Charles Pennington and the Channel Six News team arrived to cover the story. Danny raced over and leapt into his delighted father's arms.

"It's OK, Dad, really," he said happily. "Everything's going to be fine from now on."

Charles looked sheepishly at April.

"You must understand," he muttered awkwardly. "My hands were tied. But I need *you* to cover this. I'll give you anything you want. Anything!"

"Well, Charles," said April, revelling in the situation, "you're a tough negotiator, but, OK, I'll come back!"

She was just about to begin her report, when Casey ran up to her.

"I've been looking all over for you," he panted.

"Why, you don't need an ambulance, do you?" teased April, looking at his bruised face.

"Well, no, but . . ." Casey began.

"Then just shut up and kiss me, will you?" grinned April. "I've got a report to do."

"I *love* it when you're pushy," laughed Casey, hugging her close.

From high on the rooftop, Splinter and the Turtles looked down on the happy couple and applauded wildly.

"We were awesome, team," said Leonardo.

"Radical," agreed Michaelangelo. "Far out."

"Stupendous," added Raphael, "Simply excellent."

Donatello, momentarily lost for words, looked to Splinter for help.

"I have always liked . . ." said Splinter after a few seconds' thought, " . . .cowabunga!"

"Cowabunga!" cried the Turtles in unison and their battle cry was born!

★★★ ★★★

Radical
STUPENDOUS
AWESOME

Cowabunga!

IT'S WORSE!

THE END